To my brothers and sisters—
Ellen, Skip, Sean, Patrick, Maura, Linh
—D.D.M.

For Jerry Kalback and Doug Goldsmith,
and for Eric May, wherever you are
—C.B.

BUG PATROL

by Denise Dowling Mortensen • Illustrated by Cece Bell

SCHOLASTIC INC.

9 A.M.
Behind the wheel,
riding in
my Bug Mobile.

Coffee, cruller,
cruise control.
I'm Captain Bob,
Bug Patrol.

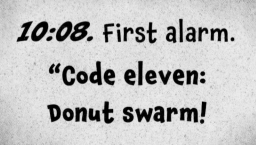

10:08. First alarm.
"Code eleven:
Donut swarm!

"Urban ants,
acting rude.
Pushing, shoving
for some food!"

WEE-O! WEE-O! WEE-O! WOO!

Bug Mobile coming through!

"Rowdy ants,
form a line.
Show your manners
when you dine!

Take a crumb,
do a deed.
Share it with
an ant in need."

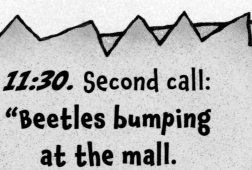

11:30. Second call:
"Beetles bumping
at the mall.

"Drivers in a parking race. Fender-bender over space!"

WEE-O!
WEE-O!
WEE-O!
WOO!

Bug Mobile coming through!

Write an
accident report.
Hand out tickets.
Tempers short.

"Naughty beetles,
give a hug.
Be patient with
your fellow bug!"

12:33.
"Speeding spiders!
Dodging traffic
on low riders.

WEE-O! WOO!

Bug Mobile coming through!

Corner spiders
in an alley.
End of motorcycle
rally.

Perpetrators
lectured, fined.
No more speeding.
Peace of mind.

Grab a wrap.
Walk my beat.

Wave hello.
Shoot the breeze.
Catch up with
the local bees.

Honey's DINER

OPEN

SAL'S PIZZA

3:15.
"Sidewalk swell.
Picket line
at Roach Hotel."

Take those roaches
for a ride,
to a place
more dignified.

Paradise ESTATES

Where food is
free and homes
are nice.
"Behold—
the Landfill Paradise!"

4:53. "Emergency!
Report of mother
missing flea.

"Doggie shook a bit too hard. Little flea lost in yard!"

WEE-O! WEE-O! WEE-O! WOO!

Bug Mobile coming through!

Use my
magnifying glass.
Find that flea
in the grass.

Cradle him
in my palm.
Keep him safe.
Call his mom.

Doggie, Mom,
and her flea.
Reunited.
Happily.

7:48.
"Investigate:
Party crickets
up too late.

"They just want to
chirp and leap.
Neighbors want
a good night's sleep!"

Megaphone
turned up high.
Play my cricket
lullaby.

Take it slow,
drive through town.
Party crickets
settle down.

8:00. Time to run.
Bug Patrolling
work is done.

Hurry home
to my nest.

And the bugs
that I love
BEST!